P9-BYQ-719

The next pitch was up a little, but Jenny swung.

Hard!

Jacob heard that solid *crack!* when she hit it.

The ball leaped off her bat and arched into right field—high and *very* long.

Jacob knew that Jenny had never actually hit one over the fence, but this one was *way* out there.

The left fielder went back . . . back . . . back. . . .

And then he looked up and watched.

The ball was twenty feet over his head . . . and *gone* for a home run.

GRAND SLAM!!!

**Look for these books
about the Angel Park All-Stars**

UP TO BAT

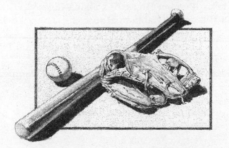

By Dean Hughes

Illustrated by Dennis Lyall

Bullseye Books • Alfred A. Knopf
New York

A BULLSEYE BOOK PUBLISHED BY ALFRED A. KNOPF
Copyright © 1991 by Dean Hughes
Cover art copyright © 1991 by Rick Ormond
Interior illustrations copyright © 1991 by Dennis Lyall
ANGEL PARK ALL-STARS characters copyright © 1989 by
Alfred A. Knopf, Inc.

All rights reserved under International and Pan-American
Copyright Conventions. Published in the United States by
Alfred A. Knopf, Inc., New York, and simultaneously in
Canada by Random House of Canada Limited, Toronto.
Distributed by Random House, Inc., New York.

Library of Congress Cataloging-in-Publication Data
Hughes, Dean, 1943–
Up to bat / by Dean Hughes ; illustrated by Dennis Lyall.
p.   cm.—(Angel Park all-stars ; 12)
"Bullseye books."
Summary: Sixth grader Jenny Roper, the Dodgers' star first
baseman, suddenly becomes concerned about her reputation
as a jock.
ISBN 0-679-81539-2 (pbk.)—ISBN 0-679-91539-7 (lib. bdg.)
[1. Baseball—Fiction. 2. Sex role—Fiction.] I. Lyall, Dennis,
ill. II. Title. III. Series: Hughes, Dean, 1943– Angel Park
all-stars ; 12.
PZ7.H87312Up   1991
[Fic]—dc20   90-49583

RL: 4.7
First Bullseye Books edition: June 1991
Manufactured in the United States of America
10 9 8 7 6 5 4 3 2 1

for Reed Tyler

★1★

Jenny's Day

Coach Wilkens stood with his hands tucked in his back pockets. He was looking down at the Dodger players. They were sitting on the grass, near the third-base line. In a few minutes their big game with the Mariners would be starting.

"Well, kids," he said, "we finished in second place for the first half of the season. Are you satisfied with that?"

"No," the players mumbled.

Above the others Sterling Malone, the center fielder, shouted, *"No way! Second stinks.* We're the best team in the league."

"Well, then, what do you plan to do about it?" the coach asked.

Jonathan Swingle answered for everyone.

"We'll take first in the second half and then beat the Giants for the championship. We're going all the way!"

"That's right. *All the way!*" Henry White repeated.

And then the whole team picked it up. *"All the way! All the way! All the way!"*

Jacob Scott loved what he was hearing. The Dodgers were finally coming together. He was only a fourth grader, but he wanted to help win that championship.

In practice he had been *stinging* the ball, and that's what he planned to do today!

"Okay. Great," the coach said. "We have the most talented team in the league, and I think it's time we *show it!*"

The players cheered, and Billy Bacon yelled, "Let's kick the Mariners' butts all the way back to San Lorenzo!"

As the kids got up Jenny Roper said, "Let's jump on them in the first inning! Let's get some runs!"

And jump on them they did.

Lian Jie, the Taiwanese player, did what he always did best. He punched a little drive straight up the middle for a single.

Then Henry slammed a double in the left-center gap, and Lian scored all the way from first.

Just like that, the Dodgers were on top, one-zip.

As usual, Jacob began his "broadcast" of the game. "Well, Hank, the Dodgers have come out swinging."

"Yup, Frank, that Mariner pitcher may want to wear his helmet out there. He's got some real *bullets* flying around him."

Sterling took hold of Jacob's fist—the one Jacob used for his "microphone." He pulled it close to his own mouth and said, "Here's a little prediction, Hank . . . or Frank . . . whichever one you are."

"Both," Jacob said, grinning and showing the split between his front teeth.

"Well, anyway, here's my prediction. I'm gonna hit a shot over the fence, over the desert . . . and halfway to China."

"Now, son," Jacob said as he pulled his fist back, "don't lie to me. That ball won't make it past downtown L.A."

Kenny Sandoval, the best fourth-grade player in the league—maybe the best *player* in the league—was stepping up to bat.

"Bring Henry home!" Jacob yelled to his friend.

Kenny started to swing but then held up on a pitch outside. Kenny stepped out of the box, adjusted his batting gloves, and stepped back in. He looked ready!

Jacob was sure that Kenny would have no trouble with Smagler, the pitcher. The kid was a good player—as an infielder—but he didn't have a strong enough arm to handle the Dodgers.

Kenny took another pitch, low, and then he got one down the middle, and he drilled it.

The shortstop got in front of it, but it almost knocked his feet out from under him. It shot off the kid's shoe and rolled toward third base.

Henry had to hold at second, and Kenny was on with a single.

That meant "Swat" Swingle was up. If Kenny wasn't the best player in the league, Swat probably was.

But he got no chance to prove it this time.

Poor Smagler was scared by now. He moved the ball around pretty well. The only trouble was, he never put it in the strike zone.

Swingle walked on four pitches.

And that brought up Sterling—and his prediction.

No one let him forget it either.

All the Dodgers teased him, but they wanted him to crack a long one—and they knew he could.

It was a warm, very still Saturday morning in Angel Park. The Mariners and their fans were suddenly quiet. They must have felt, already, that a disaster was coming.

Sterling hiked his bat high, held still as a statue.

And waited.

Waited.

Then he got his pitch!

He let loose with everything he had. He *lashed* at the ball, tried to *murder* it—tried to knock it off the planet.

But he barely ticked it.

The ball trickled off his bat and dribbled down the third-base line—like a good bunt.

The third baseman charged. The pitcher hurried over. But the only hope was for it to roll foul.

And for a time it seemed it would. Then, at the last second, it took a little turn away from the line and rolled to a stop.

Henry scored from third, and the bases were still loaded.

And by now the Dodgers were all over Sterling!

Everyone had something to say about his "power" hitting.

Sterling laughed and yelled back, "Hey, that was a perfect bunt—and an RBI. What do you want?"

Billy wouldn't let up. "Hey, Malone," he yelled, "if that's all the power you've got, maybe you ought to play in a *girls'* league."

But that was the wrong thing to say!

Jenny Roper was on her way to the plate, and she spun around. "Watch it!" she said. "You want to see some *girl* power? I'll show you."

She was smiling, but Jacob knew she meant it.

Billy didn't say a word. Jenny was one of the team's best hitters.

Jenny stepped into the box and dug in. She swung her bat, taking easy cuts until the pitcher came set. Then she pulled the bat back and assumed her left-handed stance.

Her back heel came up just a little, and she leaned in toward the plate. She held the bat steady, the way the coach had taught the players to do.

The first pitch was wide, and Jenny let it go. But she had followed it closely. Jacob could see that she had wanted to go after it.

The next pitch was up a little, but Jenny swung.

Hard!

Jacob heard that solid *crack!* when she hit it.

The ball leaped off her bat and arched into right field—high and *very* long.

Jacob knew that Jenny had never actually hit one over the fence, but this one was *way* out there.

The left fielder went back . . . back . . . back. . . .

And then he looked up and watched.

The ball was twenty feet over his head . . . and *gone* for a home run.

GRAND SLAM!!!

The whole team went crazy.

And Jenny forgot to trot. She almost ran over the top of Jonathan Swingle before she realized that she could take her time and enjoy herself.

By the time she jumped on home plate with both feet, the team was waiting for her. "That's *girl* power," she said to Billy, and she shook her fist.

Billy grinned back at her. "That's just plain *power*," he said. And he could have added that he had never hit a baseball that far in his life.

The team was on a roll now. Billy got a hit of his own—although it was only a little blooper of a single that Jenny teased him about.

And Jacob was right about being ready to sting the ball today. He laced a double into right field that scored Billy.

By the time the top of the first inning was over, the Dodgers were up 7 to 0, and they were feeling great.

Then Swingle went out and shut the Mariners down in the bottom of the inning.

And that's the way the game kept going. At the end of five innings the Dodgers were ahead 12 to 0.

Jenny had two more hits and another RBI—five for the day. Jonathan pounded a two-run homer, and Kenny had three hits himself.

Anthony Ruiz replaced Jacob in the fourth, but Jacob was two for two, so he was feeling great.

Things really couldn't have been much better.

The Dodgers were unstoppable.

And then something very strange happened.

★ 2 ★

Spectator Sport

With some kids you never know what they're going to do. But not Jenny Roper. Jacob always knew what to expect from Jenny. She was one member of the team you could *always* rely on.

Or at least that's what Jacob thought.

And then, as the team was warming up for the bottom of the fifth inning, Jacob witnessed something he wouldn't have believed if he hadn't seen it with his own eyes.

Jenny was taking throws from the infielders. She seemed relaxed, and she was talking it up, shouting, "Good throw, Henry!" and "Way to chuck it, Kenny!"

Everything was normal.

And then Jacob heard a voice from the sidelines. "Hey, Jenny."

The sound started low but tailed off into a squeak. Jacob could tell that the guy's voice was changing.

Jacob saw a kid he recognized standing close to the chain-link fence, near first base. He was a guy named Carl Adams.

Carl was a junior high student now, but Jacob knew him from elementary school the year before. He was tall and skinny, and sort of ordinary, as far as Jacob was concerned. But he remembered that a lot of girls talked about how "cute" he was.

Jacob was surprised that Carl would be saying hello to Jenny, but he was a lot more surprised by what he saw Jenny do.

She turned around, said "Hi" rather softly, and then blushed bright red.

It was the first time Jacob had ever seen her do anything like that.

Jacob *knew* Jenny was a girl. He even knew she was cute—or at least he thought so when he saw her at school. Still, he never thought much about her being a girl when the team was out on the field.

But here she was looking at a boy and blushing. She even seemed sort of shy—and Jenny just *wasn't* a shy person.

And then she dropped a throw from Lian.

Jenny *never* dropped an easy throw like that!

Something was going on.

"Hey, Jenny, I hear you're *real* good." The voice ended in a squeak again. Maybe Carl was nervous.

Michael Wilkens, the assistant coach, was standing near the fence. He said, "She's not good; she's *great*. You should have seen the home run she hit in the first inning."

"Really? Over the fence?"

Jenny's ears were so red they were like beacon lights sticking out from under her cap.

"Over the fence and *out of town*," Michael said. "We still haven't found the ball."

Jenny looked as though she wanted to crawl under first base and hide. She was standing up straight as the foul line, stiff, not on her toes—even though Swat was getting ready to pitch.

Jacob was worried. He was actually relieved when Jonathan struck out the first batter. He wasn't sure Jenny could have made a play.

The next batter, the second baseman, stayed with one of Jonathan's curve balls and knocked it between Henry and Kenny into left field.

Eddie Boschi charged the ball, but it hopped up on him and hit his shoulder. By the time Eddie got to the ball and made the throw, the runner was on second.

All the Dodgers talked it up, yelled to Jonathan to get tough on Cisco, the lead-off batter.

Jenny wasn't saying a word. Jacob saw her glance to her left now and then, and he knew she was checking to see if Carl was still there.

He was.

And that's probably what caused the problem.

"Hey, batta, batta, batta," the infield chanted. *"SWING!"*

Cisco did. He hit a two-hop grounder right to Kenny at shortstop. Kenny looked the runner back to second, and then *gunned* the ball to first.

But Jenny tripped as she moved to the base. She dropped to her knees but made a wild stab at the ball. She knocked it down and kept it from rolling away, but the runner was safe.

Jacob couldn't believe it!

This new person playing first base was not the Jenny that Jacob had watched for a season and a half.

As it turned out, the mistake didn't cause any real problems. Jonathan struck out the next batter and then got Cast, the center fielder, to hit an easy fly to right. Anthony Ruiz—a third grader—was playing right field now, and Jacob feared the worst, but Anthony camped under the ball and made the catch.

Anthony looked very happy as he ran back to the dugout, but Jenny was moving like a mummy in one of those old horror movies. The girl had forgotten how to walk, it seemed.

"What's with Jenny?" Jonathan asked as he came into the dugout. "Does she like that guy over there or something?"

Jacob, of course, had been thinking the same thing. But he wondered: Could love— or whatever it was—really do that much damage?

Jenny was up to bat first in the inning. She was three-for-three for the day, on a real *hot* streak.

But it was the new Jenny who walked to the plate. She stepped into the box and stood there stiff, like one of those grandmas in a really old photograph.

She took an awkward swing and clunked the ball, one bounce, straight back to the pitcher.

She didn't even run right.

Jacob was just glad the game wasn't on the line.

As it turned out, Jenny's sudden change

didn't matter very much. Harlan Sloan, Jacob's other good friend from the fourth grade, got a single, and then Anthony got his second hit of the season.

When Ben Riddle drove in a run, everyone got excited for the young players and sort of forgot about Jenny.

And she did seem to unwind a little after that. She made two put-outs in the sixth, and even though she didn't look quite as natural as usual, she got the job done.

The Dodgers had their victory, 13 to 0, and no harm was done.

All the same, Jacob hoped that Carl wasn't planning to come to the rest of the games that season.

Once all the congratulations and hand slaps were finished, most of the players ran to the coach's van for sodas. Jenny walked over to the fence and talked to Carl.

Jacob didn't plan to listen. But his mother called him over, and she had also come down to the fence. While she gave him instructions about the family schedule for the day,

Jacob was actually tuned in to the conversation going on a few yards away.

"So you really hit a home run?" Carl was asking.

"Yeah." And then Jenny said something else, very softly. It sounded like "phst un" to Jacob.

"What?"

"It was my first one."

"You're really good."

Another mumble: "Um mist op."

"What?"

"I messed up a couple of times."

"Not really."

Love sounded pretty stupid, Jacob told himself.

Then some other guy came walking up. He seemed to be a buddy of Carl's.

"Hey, come on. Let's go," he said.

Carl nodded, and he said good-bye to Jenny. But as he started to walk away, his friend said, "Is that the girl you were telling me about?" Carl said nothing, but the friend looked back at Jenny and said, "Hey, I hear you're *some* jock. You've probably got bigger muscles than Carl does."

Jacob's mom was giving some sort of warning to Jacob about what he could and couldn't eat from the refrigerator, but he missed the whole thing. He was watching Jenny, who was now turning white as an iceberg, as if she were either going to faint or clobber someone.

Instead, she turned and started to walk away at the same time Jacob did, so that they ended up shoulder to shoulder heading in the same direction.

"Good game," Jacob said, just trying to think of something to say.

"I'm quitting," Jenny said. "I am. I'm quitting."

"Quitting what?"

"Baseball."

"What?"

But Jenny had started to run, and one thing Jacob knew for sure was that he could never keep up with her.

So he kept walking. But he felt as though

a ball of lead had dropped into his stomach. If this skinny Carl guy was going to ruin the Angel Park Dodgers' chances for the championship, Jacob was going to *boing* the guy with one of their aluminum bats!

BOX SCORE, GAME 11

Angel Park Dodgers 13   San Lorenzo Mariners 0

	ab	r	h	rbi		ab	r	h	rbi
Jie 2b	3	1	2	0	Cisco lf	2	0	0	0
White 3b	5	1	2	2	Smagler p	1	0	0	0
Sandoval ss	4	3	3	0	Cast cf	3	0	1	0
Swingle p	3	3	2	3	Rodriguez 1b	3	0	1	0
Malone cf	4	1	1	1	Sullivan 3b	3	0	1	0
Roper 1b	4	1	3	5	Korman c	3	0	1	0
Boschi lf	4	0	0	0	Watson rf	1	0	0	0
Bacon c	2	1	1	0	Bernhardt ss	1	0	0	0
Scott rf	2	1	2	1	Klein 2b	2	0	1	0
Sloan c	2	1	1	0	Rondeau rf	2	0	0	0
Ruiz rf	2	0	1	0	Casper p	1	0	0	0
Riddle 2b	2	0	1	1	Ford ss	1	0	0	0
ttl	**37**	**13**	**19**	**13**		**23**	**0**	**5**	**0**

Dodgers   7 2 1   0 2 1—13
Mariners 0 0 0   0 0 0—0

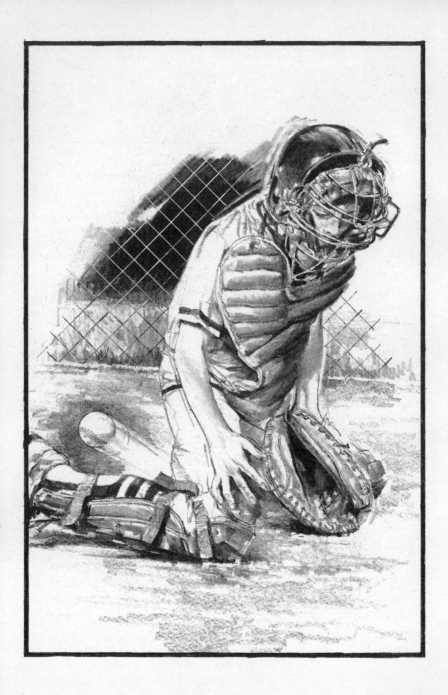

★ 3 ★

No Show

That night Jacob got a phone call. He was surprised when his big sister said, "Jacob, it's for you, and . . . ooh-*ooooh* . . . it's a *girl!*"

Jacob told his sister to get lost, and he took the phone. He recognized Jenny's voice immediately. "Jacob, did you tell anyone what I said after the game today—about quitting?"

"Well, yeah. I told Kenny and Harlan."

"I was afraid of that."

"You're not really quitting, are you?"

"I don't know." Jenny paused for a few seconds. "Look, Jacob, I talked to the coach just now. I might quit, and I might not. He wants me to think it over. But I don't want anyone else on the team to know until I decide."

"Okay. I'll call Kenny and Harlan and tell them not to say anything. But Jenny, if you quit, we'll *never* win the championship. We need you."

"I don't know, Jacob," Jenny said. "It probably wouldn't make that much difference. I'm sort of . . . losing interest in baseball."

"But why, Jenny?"

"I don't know. It's just getting kind of weird to be the only girl on the team. It didn't used to bother me. I guess I'm getting interested in some other things."

Jacob knew what that meant. Carl was one of those "things." He also knew that she hadn't liked being called a "jock."

"Jenny, it's okay for girls to be good at sports."

"I know. I just . . . well, I just have to think about it."

"You shouldn't listen to what that jerk said.

He probably couldn't hit a fastball if he swung a barn door."

But Jenny didn't want to talk about it. "Anyway," she finally said, "I've got to decide in the next few days what I'm going to do. The coach wants me to keep playing, but he said he'll support me, no matter what I decide."

Jacob made one last try: "Jenny, we still have a good chance for the championship. And then you could quit after that."

"Yeah, I know. But if we did that and then went to the district tournament, the season would stretch out into the summer. I'm thinking maybe I want to get involved in some other stuff. There's probably someone good who could come up from the minor league and play with you guys."

Jacob didn't think so. Not anyone as good as Jenny. But he didn't want her to feel rotten either, so he let her go.

And then he called his friends. They both had the same opinion about Jenny. She was getting interested in guys, and she was afraid they wouldn't like her if she was better at sports than they were. But that was a *lousy* reason to quit playing.

Besides, the Dodgers *needed* Jenny.

They found that out for sure on Wednesday.

The Dodgers were playing the Reds. When the time came for the game to start, Jenny wasn't there. The coach watched for her right up until game time, and then he sent Harlan out to first base to play for her.

When Jonathan asked where Jenny was, Coach Wilkens didn't say anything about her quitting. In fact, he said, "I'm not sure. I thought she would be here."

Harlan played pretty well, but everyone kept watching for Jenny. Something was very different without her. The team seemed flat.

Jenny had always fired up the other players—not only with her bat and her skills at first but with her attitude. She believed the team could win even if they got a few runs down. And then she would go out and get the hit to get things started.

Kenny was pitching, and he looked good

in the first inning. But in the second he walked the first batter. Jon Higdon, the Reds' shortstop, then hit a roller to Jonathan, and the Dodgers should have had an easy force at second.

But Jonathan's throw was high. Lian jumped for it and knocked it down, but the runner was safe.

Jacob was nervous.

He would have almost been happier if Jonathan had thrown one of his temper tantrums. Instead, Jonathan shook his head and walked back to his position.

Where was that old Dodger *fire?*

The next batter blasted a shot all the way to the fence, and two runs scored.

Kenny got the bottom of the order out and held the score to two-nothing, but the Dodgers couldn't even get a runner on base again in the bottom of the inning. Gerstein was throwing hard, and his control was perfect.

Jacob could see trouble ahead. He found himself looking across the park, watching for Jenny.

Some of the guys were not so patient. "What's with Jenny?" Jonathan demanded. "Does anyone know where the heck she is?"

Jacob had just made the final out of the second inning and was coming back for his glove. He kept his mouth shut.

The team ran out to the field. All the players were yelling, saying all the right things, but they didn't sound very convincing.

And that meant trouble. The Reds were too good. They didn't need any help to get runs.

The lead-off batter popped up, but then Schulman, the big catcher, hit a shot down the first-base line. Harlan dove at the ball but couldn't get it.

Jacob hurried over and made a good throw, holding Schulman to a double. But as Jacob trotted back to his position he was thinking what everyone else must have been thinking: Jenny might have gotten to the ball. She was quicker than Harlan, and had better hands.

Gerstein then powered a drive into deep

center that Sterling had to go way back for. Schulman tagged up and loped over to third.

With two outs Jacob was hoping they could hold the Reds. But Kenny wasn't quite as sharp as usual. The Reds were getting good wood on the ball.

Kenny looked disgusted with himself. He tried to put something extra on the next pitch. It was a hard curve, but it came in low and then broke into the dirt.

Billy tried to block the pitch with his body, but as he dropped to the ground the ball shot between his knees.

The run scored from third.

Kenny did get the batter after that, but now the score was 3 to 0.

The Dodgers had to get something going!

Jonathan fumed and shouted as the Dodgers got back to the dugout. "Who's going to start *hitting* the ball?" he yelled. "Come on, Eddie, get on base."

But Eddie struck out. And Billy hit a soft grounder. And Harlan fouled off a couple of pitches and then took a terrible swing at a big curve.

Strike three.

The Dodgers were heading back to the field. And Gerstein had retired the first nine batters in order.

"What's the matter with you guys?" he taunted as he walked from the mound. "Am I just *too much* for you?"

"Shut up, Gerstein!" Billy yelled. "Just wait until next inning."

Gerstein didn't like that. He shook a finger at Billy and said, "I'm going to no-hit you guys. The mighty Dodgers are getting *nothing* off me today."

Schulman was standing near the dugout, taking his catcher's gear off. "Hey, that won't be tough, Jimmy," he yelled to Gerstein. "Swat thinks he's *bad,* and so does Sandoval. But their best hitter is a *girl,* and she's not even here today."

"Shut up, Schulman," Jonathan yelled.

Coach Wilkens stepped in. "That's enough, boys," he told them. "Let's play ball."

Still, when Jacob got to right field, he turned around and scanned the park. Was

Jenny going to show up? He could pretty well guess that the worst had happened. She had decided to quit and just hadn't worked up the nerve to tell the coach yet.

Jacob knew that Schulman wasn't exactly right. Jenny wasn't the best hitter on the team. But she was *one* of the best.

And without her the Dodgers' chance to win the championship was probably gone.

★ **4** ★

Now or Never

The Reds didn't score in the fourth.

But the Dodgers still weren't doing anything either.

Gerstein got the first two Dodger batters and kept his string going—eleven batters in a row.

But now Kenny was coming up to bat. He dug in and got set. His eyes were like bullets. Jacob knew he meant business.

Gerstein played it smart. He changed up on the first pitch. Kenny had been expecting smoke, and he swung way early and fouled the pitch off.

"Pound this next one!" Jonathan shouted from the on-deck area. "Get on base and I'll bring you home."

Jacob was guessing fastball. Everyone was. But Gerstein threw an off-speed curve. Kenny backed away, and the ball broke over the plate for a second strike.

"*Come on!*" Jonathan pleaded. "You can hit Gerstein. You've hit him all year."

Kenny stepped out of the box and took a long breath. Jacob was sure the fastball was coming now. And Kenny would be ready.

But Gerstein stayed with his slow stuff, and Kenny guessed wrong. He was way off stride. He reached for the ball, lamely, and missed.

Strikeout!

Twelve outs in a row. A perfect game after four innings.

Kenny slammed his bat on the ground—something he almost never did.

Gerstein laughed and yelled, "What's the matter, Sandoval? Can't you hit my *junk?*"

The whole Reds' bench was pouring it on. "Jimmy's going to shut you out, Dodgers," they were yelling. "You guys are getting *no* hits today."

Kenny marched to the mound.

But he didn't lose his cool. He threw hard. His control was getting sharper as the game went along.

He put away the first two batters with no trouble.

And he should have had the third.

Schulman knocked a little fly toward left. Lian went back, but the sun got in his eyes, and he lost it for a second. He recovered enough to stab at the ball, but it hit off the heel of his glove and dropped to the grass.

That brought Gerstein to the plate.

Jacob wondered what Kenny would do. Maybe he would try Gerstein's tricks and come with a change-up.

But no way. Kenny went to his fastball, on the outside and at the knees. Gerstein swung and missed.

He then came inside, and Gerstein took the pitch for a ball.

But that was the setup pitch for a big curve that started inside and broke. Gerstein began to move out of the way and then must have seen the spin of the ball. He tried to swing too late, and he fouled the pitch off.

Now the Dodgers were giving the business to Gerstein.

But that only made him mad. He was ready when the next pitch came. And he swung hard.

This time Kenny *did* change up.

Swing and a miss!

Strike three!

The Dodgers cheered, and Gerstein threw his bat on the ground and then kicked it.

And as the Dodgers came charging back to the dugout Jacob thought he sensed a new mood. Maybe this would be the turning point.

Sure, they could use Jenny. But maybe she was gone for the season, and the team would have to come through without her. They couldn't let any one player be all that important.

The best news was that Swat was starting off the bottom of the fifth. Not many pitchers could keep him off base for a whole game.

Gerstein didn't look quite so cocky either. He needed six outs to finish his no-hitter, but he knew he was probably facing the toughest batter right now.

Jonathan acted as though he wanted to hit the ball out of sight. He took some hard practice swings and then set himself in that powerful position of his, his big arms held high.

But he did the last thing anyone expected. Gerstein went to his off-speed stuff once too often. Jonathan squared off and had no trouble laying a bunt down the third-base line.

The ball rolled slowly down the line, and with Jonathan's speed, the Reds had no chance. But the third baseman grabbed the ball and threw anyway.

That was a big mistake.

He tossed the ball over the first baseman's head, and Jonathan ended up on second.

Gerstein stood on the mound, facing Jonathan. He had his hands on his hips. "No guts, huh, Swingle?" he shouted. "You didn't dare try to *hit* my pitches."

"Hey, I hit it—right where I wanted to,"

Jonathan said, grinning. "And your no-hitter is *dead*."

Schulman was yelling from behind the plate. "Hey, why do they call you *Swat*? They ought to call you *Sweetie pie*. That was a *girl's* trick."

All the Reds picked up on that one. "Yeah," one of the Reds yelled, "they don't have Jenny today, so Jonathan has to make up for it."

Jonathan had been happy to get on base. But he didn't like this kind of stuff.

The ump finally put a stop to it, but Jonathan was mad. Jacob could see that he was still talking—loud enough for Gerstein to hear even if the umpire couldn't.

Tempers were getting hot. Jacob just hoped that the Dodgers would use that to their advantage.

Gerstein looked as upset as anyone. And that showed up on his first pitch to Sterling. It was high and hard—way out of the strike zone.

Schulman yelled to him not to overthrow, but Gerstein was still mad, and he threw hard again. This time he threw a curve that hung over the plate. Sterling smacked the ball into center field.

Jonathan took off with the crack of the bat and was going full speed as he hit third base.

But Coach Wilkens had both arms in the air, and he was shouting, "Hold up."

Jacob understood that. The Dodgers needed three runs, not one, and there was no use taking a chance on . . .

But Jonathan wasn't stopping. He steamed right on past the coach.

The center fielder grabbed the ball on one bounce and fired it home. It was a good throw, and Schulman was in front of the plate waiting for it.

Jonathan was coming hard and saw Schulman take the throw. But Jonathan didn't slide. He lowered a shoulder and hit Schulman with a pounding body block.

Schulman was huge, but Jonathan was big too, and he was really traveling. He sent Schulman flying.

And the ball flipped straight into the air.

Jonathan scored, and Sterling went to second.

And then Jonathan jumped up and pointed a finger in Schulman's face. "Now tell me if you think I'm a *girl*," he screamed.

The Dodgers cheered.

But the Reds were all running out toward home plate, and the Dodgers, seeing that, all charged out too.

Both umpires had to jump in the middle of it all and stop things from getting out of hand. No one threw any punches, but the mood was ugly.

"All right, boys," the home plate ump yelled. "One more outbreak like this and I'll cancel the game and put both teams down for a loss. We won't have this kind of stuff."

"That's right," Coach Wilkens said. "Jonathan, go sit down. I'm taking you out of the game."

But the Reds' coach didn't pull anyone, and the Dodgers didn't like that. The mood was still angry when Jacob walked to the plate. He expected the first pitch to be right under his chin.

Gerstein played it smart, however. He threw his curve.

Jacob bailed out, and all the Reds laughed.

But Jacob wasn't going to let that happen again.

The next pitch was hard, and Gerstein probably meant it to be inside. All the same, it was out over the plate, and Jacob took a level stroke and drove the ball right past Gerstein's ear and on into center field.

This time Sterling obeyed the coach and stopped at third. The tying runs were on, and the Dodgers had their chance.

Jacob knew that the team had to come through *right now*. They may not get another opportunity like this in the final inning.

Besides, something else was going on and everyone knew it.

The Dodgers had to prove to themselves that they could win without Jenny.

★ 5 ★

Trouble

Eddie Boschi was up to bat.

Two on. And the Dodgers were two runs down.

No outs.

This was it.

But Gerstein knew that too. He had lost his no-hitter and his shutout. Now he had to settle down and get the win. Jacob could see in his face that he had made up his mind to do just that.

He took his time, seemed to talk to himself, and then he made a perfect pitch, hard and away from Eddie. Eddie reached for it and hit the ball on the ground toward the right side.

With no outs Coach Wilkens didn't take

the chance. He held Sterling at third. The Reds' second baseman fielded the grounder and went for the force at second.

Runners were still at the corners. But now there was an out.

Billy walked to the plate. He turned and waved a doubled fist to his dugout.

But the Reds were really on him. Billy took a couple of close ones and got ahead of the pitcher, but then he swung over a pitch and topped the ball.

It bounced toward third.

Sterling had to hold again. The third baseman threw to second for another force.

Runners *still* at the corners.

But two outs.

The Reds' confidence came soaring back. The infielders really talked it up. "No problem," Schulman bellowed. "Two down, and a weak hitter coming up."

The "weak hitter" was Harlan.

The truth was, he probably was the weakest hitter in the starting lineup that day. And the other truth—the one that Jacob hardly liked to think about—was that he was up to bat because Jenny wasn't there.

If only . . .

But Jacob didn't want to think that way about his good friend. Harlan could come through. Jenny was a good hitter, but Harlan could be tough too, and he had proved it plenty of times.

Harlan didn't seem scared. He had come a long way since his early games the year before. He was tall and still sort of awkward-looking when he swung, but he had learned to control his bat, to watch the pitch, to meet the ball.

He had also learned to make the pitcher get the ball over the plate.

Gerstein powered the first pitch—*bam*—into Schulman's mitt. But the umpire called it a ball.

"What are you talking about, ump?" Gerstein yelled. "That pitch was in there."

"Just pitch. I'll call 'em," the big umpire called back to him.

The next pitch was in the strike zone, and this time Harlan *met* it. He stroked it hard to left field.

Jacob jumped to the dugout fence and watched the ball soar long and deep. The left fielder was running almost straightway from the plate, since Harlan had *murdered* the ball.

The left fielder got to the fence in time and waited.

Jacob began to scream in his radio-broadcast voice, "That ball is way back. *Way* back. It's going . . . *going* . . ."

And then the left fielder reached up and caught the ball.

The Reds all charged in and surrounded Gerstein as though the game were over.

The Dodgers wouldn't accept that. They kept telling each other they still had another inning. They could still do it.

That's what they said. But something inside said to Jacob, "We had our chance. We didn't do it."

The same voice must have been speaking to everyone.

The Reds, with new confidence, got two more runs in the top of the sixth. And the Dodgers went out easily in the bottom of the inning.

That was the game. And the Dodgers'

chances to win the championship had taken a serious blow.

Maybe a deathblow! The second half was just starting, but the Giants had been rolling over everyone all season. The Dodgers were the only team with much chance of beating them. But that meant the Dodgers shouldn't be losing to anyone else.

When it was all over and the Dodgers had listened to all the gloating they could take, they walked over to the coach's van. Before he gave them their soft drinks—which no one cared much about anyway—he told them he wanted to talk to them.

"Listen, kids," he told the players. "I don't want you to get down on yourselves. You played a great game. Harlan gave the ball a real ride. Another few inches and he would have put us on top, and then we might have gotten them."

Most of the kids were looking down at the grass.

Jacob knew what everyone was thinking. What the coach said was true. But it didn't change anything. They had still lost.

They had all thought this was going to be their big year. And now the championship was slipping away.

"Jonathan," the coach said, "I hope you understood why I took you out of the game. Two reasons." He didn't sound exactly mad—just firm. "First, you ran right through my signal. A team can't operate that way.

"And second, there's nothing wrong with colliding with a guy when he's blocking the plate on you. But that taunting stuff—yelling in his face like that—I don't like. That's not baseball."

"He called me a *girl*, coach. I had to show him."

The coach stood and looked at Jonathan for several seconds before he finally said, "Well, now, Jonathan, that's interesting. A little earlier you were mad because a *girl* didn't show up to play today. If that kid was saying you play like Jenny, I'd say he was giving you a *compliment*."

"Yeah, well, where was she?"

Jonathan was changing the subject, but it was a good question.

Coach Wilkens only said, "I don't know. But you let *me* deal with that. I'm sure she had a good reason."

That's what Jacob hoped.

That night Jacob decided to find out what was going on. He called Jenny. She had talked to him about her worries. Now maybe he could try to convince her to come back.

But when he got her on the phone and asked whether she had decided to quit, her answer surprised him. "Not exactly," she said. "But now I guess I *can't* come back. Everyone probably hates me."

"What are you talking about, Jenny?"

"Jacob, I don't have a good excuse for not being there. I don't know what to tell all the players."

"Look, we need you back. We lost today."

"I know. I saw the end of the game."

"*What*? Why didn't you come and play?"

"I don't know. It's stupid."

He waited, and she finally did try to explain.

"I was getting ready for the game and

these friends of mine came by. They were going to the mall, and they . . . well, they were going to meet some guys. And this one boy I thought I liked was going to be there."

"Carl?"

"Yeah. But that's not exactly . . ." Jacob listened to a long silence before Jenny finally said, "It was dumb what happened. My friends started saying I was stupid to be playing baseball with a bunch of grade school boys when I could be with junior high boys. And then one of my friends said I was never going to have any boyfriends if I kept playing boys' baseball."

"Jenny, that's stupid. There's no reason—"

"I know. I know. But I let those guys talk me into going with them. I got to thinking I was going to quit anyway, and I'd tell the coach after the game."

"Then why did you come over to the park?"

Jenny let out a long breath. She sounded mad at herself. "I don't know. I got out to the mall, and I started feeling like the biggest jerk in the world. I knew I'd let the team down. The only thing those kids were doing was giggling and acting stupid, and all I could think of was that I wanted to be at the game."

"I didn't see you—and I was watching for you."

"I know. I stayed way back—outside the right field fence by the bike racks—and I watched." Jenny's voice cracked just a little. "It almost killed me when we lost. Maybe if I'd played, we could have . . . I don't know."

"We *would* have won with you there, Jenny."

"Maybe. But I can't come back now. I can just hear what Jonathan must have said about me."

Jacob couldn't argue that one.

And he couldn't convince Jenny to come back, although he tried.

When he finally hung up the phone, he felt sick about what was going to happen to the team.

But he also thought it was a big, stupid mess that ought to be straightened out.

The only trouble was, he had no idea what he could do.

BOX SCORE, GAME 12

Cactus Hills Reds 5   Angel Park Dodgers 1

	ab	r	h	rbi		ab	r	h	rbi
Trulis 2b	3	0	0	0	Jie 2b	2	0	0	0
Schulman c	2	1	1	0	White 3b	3	0	1	0
Gerstein p	3	0	0	0	Sandoval p	3	0	0	0
Rutter 3b	2	2	1	0	Swingle ss	2	1	1	0
Higdon ss	2	2	1	0	Malone cf	2	0	1	1
Young lf	3	0	1	2	Scott rf	2	0	1	0
Bonthuis 1b	1	0	0	0	Boschi lf	2	0	0	0
Lum rf	1	0	0	0	Bacon c	2	0	0	0
Harrison cf	1	0	0	0	Sloan 1b	2	0	0	0
Hileman rf	2	0	2	2	Riddle 2b	1	0	0	0
Alfini cf	2	0	0	0	Ruiz rf	1	0	0	0
Charles 1b	2	0	0	0					
ttl	24	5	6	4		22	1	4	1

Reds   0 2 1   0 0 2—5
Dodgers   0 0 0   0 1 0—1

★ 6 ★

Deeper Trouble

On Saturday the Dodgers played the A's. No matter what Jenny had told him, Jacob kept watching for her right up until game time. He knew she was embarrassed, but he thought she might forget all that and come anyway.

But she didn't.

Jonathan said he didn't care. If she didn't want to be on the team, why should they beg her? The Dodgers could still win the championship without her.

And Jonathan did make the A's look bad that day. The Dodgers gave up two runs, but that was only because of a couple of errors. Jonathan pitched well enough to get a shutout.

But that was the good news. The A's were the worst team in the league, and somehow, the Dodgers couldn't get much offense going against them. The Dodgers won, 4 to 2, but no one felt very good after the game. They just hadn't played the way they knew they could.

And the next game went even worse.

The game was with the Padres. They were better than the A's, but they shouldn't be good enough to give the Dodgers much trouble.

But trouble was what they got.

Eddie Boschi pitched, and he did pretty well, but "Bad News" Roberts could do no wrong. He socked a three-run homer in the third inning and drove in another run in the fifth.

The worst part was, he was pitching tough, too. The Dodgers couldn't get much of anything going.

Twice Harlan came up with runners in scoring position, and both times he grounded out. No one else came through either, but Jacob kept wondering what Jenny might have done had she been there.

Worst of all was the fifth inning.

Kenny, Jonathan, and Sterling came up with the Dodgers down by three. Roberts was throwing flames. Kenny grounded out, and so did Jonathan, and then Sterling struck out on a white-hot fastball.

When Jacob led off in the top of the sixth, he knew he had to get something started. The game was on the line, with the Padres ahead 4 to 1.

Jacob walked to the plate. He mumbled his broadcast to himself. "Hank, this young man has a big load on his shoulders."

"That's right, Frank. But he can do it. I *know* he can do it!"

And Jacob kept saying those words over and over. "I *know* I can do it!"

Brenchley, the catcher, didn't think so. "Hey, little fourth grader, you going to save the day?" he asked Jacob.

Jacob didn't answer. He concentrated on Roberts, who had just stepped to the rubber.

"The mighty Dodgers aren't so hot after all, are they?"

Jacob still didn't answer.

"You didn't think you'd ever lose to the Padres, did you?"

Now the umpire said, "That's enough." But Brenchley just laughed.

And then Jacob took a pitch right down the middle. It was a dart of a fastball, but still, he should have swung.

Was he scared of Roberts?

"Don't shake, little kid," Brenchley said, and laughed. "It'll only hurt for a little while—just two more strikes."

The next pitch was hard and outside. Jacob started to swing and then tried to hold up. But he got too far around, and the umpire called it a swinging strike.

"You're almost finished," Brenchley said. "You might as well give it a shot this time. Take your best swing."

"Hey, batta, batta, batta," the infield was chanting. And the crowd was screaming from the bleachers.

Jacob stepped out of the box. He needed to get his head straight. He had to concentrate on the pitch, and nothing else.

He took a nice, level practice swing and stepped back in.

Jacob watched Roberts nod as he took the sign, and something in his satisfied look told Jacob that Bad News was going to come with his curve.

Jacob told himself to hang in, not bail out, even if the pitch looked as though it were coming right at him.

Suddenly the pitch was humming straight at his ribs, and it took all his control not to take a dive.

But he hung in, kept his eye on it, and watched it break over the plate. He drove the bat right through the ball.

Crack!

Jacob had *crushed* the ball. It rocketed past the third baseman before he could move—and it kept going. It bounced all the way to the left field fence.

Jacob might have made it to third, but he played it safe—as the coach signaled for him to do—and stopped at second.

Jacob looked at Brenchley and nodded, very nicely. He didn't say a word, but he enjoyed the moment.

Brenchley stood with his hands on his hips. He seemed to search for something to say to Jacob, but then he let it go and yelled, "Come on, Bad News, let's finish these guys."

Roberts kicked the ground and then stepped back in. He looked mad.

The Dodgers had something going.

Things looked even better when Bad News let his temper get to him. He forced the ball and ended up walking Eddie.

And then Billy beat out an infield roller, and the bases were loaded.

But Anthony Ruiz was batting for Harlan.

He gave it his best shot, but he struck out on a tough fastball. And then Ben Riddle did the same.

Just when things had looked as if they might turn, suddenly the Dodgers were on the rocks again.

They needed three runs.

The Mariners only needed one out.

At least Henry was coming up, and he was likely to put the ball in play, not strike out.

But Henry got a little anxious. He reached for the first pitch and hit a grounder to the second baseman.

Jacob ran toward home, but he knew the

game was over. If only they had . . .

But the second baseman dropped the ball as he tried to pull it from his glove. Everyone was safe.

The poor little rookie, who had just come in to play second, looked as if he wanted to cry. He didn't need Bad News yelling at him.

But he got an earful anyway.

All Jacob could think was that the season was not ruined—not yet. And Kenny was coming up.

Bases still loaded.

Jacob watched Bad News, and he saw that the error had really bothered him. He was mad that he had to keep pitching when the game should have been over. And Jacob knew something else. No matter what he and Brenchley said, they were scared of Kenny.

Roberts looked stiff on his first pitch, and the ball soared. The second pitch was even higher, and now Roberts had to be worried about walking Kenny and facing Jonathan.

So he aimed the ball. He took something off it, and Kenny *killed* it.

But the ball was hit straight at the center

fielder, and it was staying up. The fielder charged hard. He had a good chance to get to it.

But just as he was about to go down for the ball and try to catch it off his shoe-strings, he thought better of it. He held up and tried to take the ball on one bounce.

But the ball was hit very hard. It hit the grass and flattened out.

Right under the fielder's glove!

And now the chase was on. The center fielder turned around and went after the ball. The other fielders were coming hard too, but they all had a long run.

The ball bounced and rolled toward the fence, and meanwhile, Eddie scored and Billy, with his short legs, was motoring around third. Henry was catching up fast.

The center fielder finally got to the ball and made a pretty good throw, but it was all too late. Billy crossed the plate standing up, and Henry was right behind him. And Kenny was standing on third, clenching his fists and waving them at his teammates— who were going crazy.

Bad News was screaming at his center fielder that he was the biggest idiot who ever lived. But Brenchley yelled, "Shut up, Roberts. You're the one who threw the pitch."

The trouble wasn't over for the Mariners. Jonathan stepped up and banged out another hit, driving in Kenny. And then Sterling smashed a double into right field, and Jonathan scored all the way from first.

Jacob, who had started all the fireworks, got up again. This time he ended the inning, although he gave the ball a long ride to left field.

But the damage was done. The Dodgers had a three-run lead, and they held it in the bottom of the sixth.

The season wasn't over yet!

BOX SCORE, GAME 13

Paseo A's 2

	ab	r	h	rbi
Oshima 2b	3	0	1	0
De Klein cf	3	1	1	0
Sullivan lf	1	1	1	0
Smith p	2	0	1	1
Santos c	2	0	0	0
Chavez ss	1	0	0	0
Powell 3b	3	0	0	0
Trout rf	2	0	0	0
Watrous 1b	3	0	0	0
Henegan ss	1	0	0	0
Naile p	1	0	0	0
Reilly rf	1	0	0	0
ttl	23	2	4	1

Angel Park Dodgers 4

	ab	r	h	rbi
Jie 2b	2	0	1	0
White 3b	3	2	2	0
Sandoval ss	3	1	2	1
Swingle p	2	1	1	1
Malone cf	3	0	2	2
Sloan 1b	2	0	0	0
Scott rf	3	0	1	0
Boschi lf	2	0	0	0
Bacon c	2	0	0	0
Riddle 2b	1	0	0	0
Ruiz lf	1	0	0	0
	24	4	9	4

```
A's       0 0 2  0 0 0—2
Dodgers   0 0 2  0 2 x—4
```

BOX SCORE, GAME 14

Angel Park Dodgers 7

	ab	r	h	rbi
Jie 2b	3	0	1	1
White 3b	3	1	1	0
Sandoval ss	4	1	2	3
Swingle lf	4	1	2	1
Malone cf	4	0	1	1
Scott rf	4	2	2	0
Boschi p	2	1	1	0
Bacon c	2	1	2	0
Sloan 1b	2	0	0	0
Ruiz 1b	1	0	0	0
Riddle 2b	1	0	0	0
ttl	30	7	12	6

Santa Rita Padres 4

	ab	r	h	rbi
Lundberg 2b	2	1	1	0
Jorgensen lf	3	2	2	0
Roberts p	3	1	3	4
Brenchley c	3	0	0	0
Durkin 1b	3	0	2	0
Blough 3b	2	0	0	0
Valenciano cf	3	0	0	0
Campbell rf	2	0	0	0
Palmer ss	2	0	0	0
Orosco 1b	1	0	0	0
Nakatani 3b	1	0	0	0
Rollins cf	1	0	0	0
	26	4	8	4

Dodgers 0 1 0 0 0 6—7
Padres 0 0 3 0 1 0—4

★ 7 ★

Giants in the Way

Once the Dodgers stopped celebrating, the truth seemed to hit them. They had almost lost to the Mariners. And they hadn't played well against the A's.

Sure they had won, but what was going to happen when they played the Giants?

Coach Wilkens had some things to say about that. "Kids, you came through when you had to, but I don't see you playing with the same spark you usually do. Something seems to be missing."

He put his hands in his back pockets and looked around at everyone. "I'm going to walk over to the van and get the drinks out, but I'd like you to stay here and talk things over. When you think you know what you need to do, come and tell me."

The coach walked away. He didn't tell anyone to be the leader. He just said "talk things over."

Jacob was sure he knew what the team needed, but he was only a fourth grader. He didn't feel like he could say it.

Jonathan was the first to speak up. "We just gotta get psyched about beating the Giants," he said. "We didn't really play until we *had* to today. But we can do it."

Some of the guys said, "Yeah, that's right," but there was something left unsaid, and Jacob thought maybe no one was going to say it.

Finally, Henry had the guts. "Tell the truth, you guys," he said. "We need Jenny. When we need runs, she's the one who always seems to come through."

Lian agreed. "She tells us we can win," he said.

Lian didn't know exactly how to express the idea in English, but Jacob knew what he meant. Jonathan was a leader in a way. He played well. But he was critical of everyone else. Jenny wasn't like that. She made people feel they could play the game.

"We can win without any girls on the team," Jonathan said.

"Hey, who *cares* if she's a girl or not?" Sterling shot back. "She's *good*—that's all. Harlan did okay today, but we're a better team when Jenny's playing for us."

And that's when Jacob got up the nerve to say what he had been thinking all along. "Look, I've talked to her, and I'm pretty sure she wants to play. I think she'll come back if we ask her. We could go over to her house right now and tell her we don't care what happened before. We just want her to play."

"Let's do it," Sterling said.

"*Yeah,* let's do it!" Billy shouted.

Jonathan didn't say a word.

When the players told the coach what they wanted to do, he looked pleased. "Listen, you guys," he said, "I wasn't going to force you to do anything, but I hoped this is what you would want to do—not just for the team but for Jenny."

And so the whole team walked together,

or rode their bikes, and they showed up at Jenny's. When she came out to the front steps, she looked shocked.

Sterling did the talking. "Jenny, we're playing the Giants on Saturday, and we can't beat 'em unless we have our *whole team*."

"Well, I feel stupid about—"

"We don't care about any of that. Just come and play."

Jenny looked embarrassed. But she said, "Okay."

The guys cheered, and Billy said, "We're going to *squash* those Giants."

The players always said things like that. But Jacob had the feeling this was more than talk. It really felt right to get the team back together.

As kids started leaving, Jacob walked over to Jenny. "Hey, Jenny," he said, "why don't you tell Carl to stay away?" He grinned. "You play better when he's not around."

"Don't worry. I don't even like the guy. He and his buddies still make fun of me for playing ball. So I say, forget them. I can do anything I *want* to do."

Jacob liked that.

On the way home he told Kenny and Harlan he thought things were going to be all right now. They agreed, and when they got to Kenny's house, they told Kenny's dad what had happened.

He said something that Jacob hadn't really thought about. "Jenny stuck by you guys last year when you were starting out and some of the older guys were on your backs. She's your friend. I'm glad you stuck by her."

Jacob felt good about that.

By the time Saturday came, however, Jacob was really nervous. Things had felt right on Wednesday night, but now the team had to get that spark going in the game.

The Dodgers had beaten Hausberg once this season, but he had been getting tougher all year. His control was sharp, and he was putting more heat on his fastball. But it was that curve that the Dodgers struggled with.

And the Dodgers had never had much luck keeping Dave Weight off base.

The truth was, the Giants were in first place because they were *good*, and no other reason.

Today the Dodgers had to be *better*.

But in the first inning Jacob saw what they were going to be up against. Jonathan looked sharp as he put away the first two batters. But Weight timed one of Jonathan's fastballs and drove it over Eddie's head in left field.

It went for a double.

Then Villareal, the Giants' center fielder, got a little lucky. He hit the ball off the end of his bat, and it floated like a balloon just out of Kenny's reach. It dropped in for a single, and Weight scored.

That wasn't such a big deal—one run in the first. But it was the Giants they were playing. And the Dodgers had hoped to come out smoking.

Jonathan got the third out, and Jacob felt the excitement as they headed back in to bat for the first time. The Dodgers were definitely *up* for this one.

Lian started things right. He wasn't bothered by Hausberg's curve. He poked one of his little drives to the right side, and he was on with a single. Henry hit the ball on the ground and Lian was forced at second, but then Kenny stroked a nice line drive, and runners were at first and second for Jonathan.

Jonathan really wanted to *blast* one. Jacob could see that.

Hausberg moved the ball around and tried to catch big Swat off stride. Instead, he got himself behind and finally walked him.

The bases were loaded with only one out. This was the chance to break things wide open.

Sterling stepped up, confident, took a ball low, and then took a big swing at one of "House" Hausberg's curves and popped the ball straight in the air.

The umpire called the infield fly rule, and two were down.

Now it was up to Jenny. And Jacob liked that. This was her chance to fire up the team.

She walked to the plate as though she knew exactly what she were going to do. She pumped the bat a couple of times and then cocked her arms back.

"Don't let a pretty little *girl* beat you, House," someone yelled from the crowd.

Suddenly Jenny threw up her hand and

said, "Time-out." She stepped out of the batter's box. Jacob wondered whether she had let the yelling bother her. But Jenny had heard plenty of that kind of stuff.

She stepped back in and set herself. The pitch was high and tight. Her ponytail flipped in the air as she ducked to get out of the way, and her helmet went flying.

But the catcher caught the ball. In fact, he had gone up for it almost as though he had known where it would be.

Maybe the Giants wanted to see if Jenny could be frightened by a close pitch.

But she stepped in again, and she looked confident. The next pitch was over the plate, and she took a nice cut.

She sliced the ball hard to the left side. It would have been down the line against most players. But Weight dove and knocked the ball down. He never could have made the play at first, but he scrambled up, grabbed the ball, and stepped on third before Kenny could slide into the bag.

The inning was over.

Jacob knew Jenny had done her part. Weight had just made a great play.

But as Jacob went back to the dugout from the on-deck area to get his glove, Jonathan was coming after his glove too. "Well, Jacob, I thought she *always* came through."

"Hey, she hit the ball *hard,*" Jacob said.

"Yeah, well, that doesn't add up to any runs on the scoreboard, does it?"

"You know what your problem is, Jonathan?"

Jonathan stopped. Jacob was scared the guy was going to clobber him. "No, Jacob. Why don't you tell me?"

"You can't stand to think that anyone might be as good as you are. Especially a girl."

"What are you talking about? Jenny's not as good as I am."

"Maybe not. But she's close. And she *helps* the team more than you do. She doesn't make everyone feel lousy if they mess up."

Jonathan's lips moved, but nothing came out. He couldn't seem to find the right words to defend himself. Finally, he just said, "Shut up, Jacob," and he walked away.

★ 8 ★

Jenny's Back

No one scored in the second or third innings. But the Dodgers missed some good chances. They had runners on base both innings, but they just couldn't score.

In the third inning Jonathan doubled and Sterling walked. Jenny had another chance to drive runs in.

She didn't.

But she hit the ball hard again. She made the right fielder run a long way. She only missed a big hit by a few inches. But she flied out.

Jacob also had his chance, right after Jenny, but he popped up in foul territory.

In the top of the fourth Cooper, the

Giants' second baseman, led off. He kept fouling pitches off, and then, finally, on a three-and-two count, Jonathan walked him.

The Giants weren't bigmouths, but they were competitors. They were really talking it up in the dugout.

Hausberg was coming up.

Jonathan moved the ball in and out, and went to his curve, but he got behind, three-and-one, and then walked Hausberg.

It wasn't like Jonathan to walk two in a row.

He stood on the mound and took some deep breaths. From right field Jacob could see that he was upset with himself.

Dodero, the catcher, was coming up. He was not the best hitter on the team, but he was hard to strike out.

Jonathan came at him with a good fastball, and Dodero slapped the ball into right field.

A run scored.

The Giants were up two to nothing.

Jonathan walked back to the mound and kicked the rubber. Jacob knew he was mad

at himself. There was no one else to blame
for any of this.

Jenny trotted over to the mound and said
something.

Jacob saw Jonathan nod a couple of times.

When the next batter stepped in, Jonathan
fired the ball.

He blew away the next three batters. He
struck out two substitutes and then got
Sanchez, the starting shortstop, on a check-
swing ground ball.

Jenny grabbed the ball and stepped on
first, and then she ran over to Jonathan.
Jacob had been charging in to back up
Jenny. He was close by when he heard Jenny
say, "See what I told you. You're the best
pitcher in this league when you don't try
to be too fancy and just throw your best
stuff."

Jonathan nodded, and he jogged with
Jenny back to the dugout. "Thanks," he said,
but not very loud.

"We'll get 'em now," Jenny said.

But it didn't happen in the fourth.

Eddie, Harlan, and Lian went out one-two-three, and the Dodgers were back in the field. Time was running out.

But Jonathan was in a groove now. He got a called third strike on the left fielder, and then he struck out Weight on a fastball that *boomed* into Harlan's glove.

Villareal, the center fielder, kept looking for something to hit, and he ended up watching a third strike go by.

"Struck out the side!" Jenny yelled, and she ran over and slapped Jonathan on the back. *"This time* we get the runs."

But Henry sent a little bouncer to the second baseman, and Kenny flied out again. The fifth inning was heading down the drain, the same as all the others.

Still, Jonathan was up, and Jacob knew what he was thinking. This might be his last chance. He had to do it now.

Jonathan liked to swing for the fences, but that wasn't what the team needed. The Dodgers had to have at least two runs—not one—and they needed base runners, not a long out.

Jacob saw Jonathan choke up on the bat

a little. He let a curve go by, and then he punched one of Hausberg's fastballs up the middle for a clean single—just the way Lian always did.

And then, from first base, he yelled to Sterling, "Just poke one somewhere. Jenny will bring us in."

Sterling took an easy swing and plopped the ball over the shortstop's head.

Jonathan charged to second but then played it safe and didn't try to go to third.

That brought Jenny up to bat with the tying runs on.

"All right, Jenny," Jonathan shouted. "This is it. You can do it."

Jacob had a feeling Jenny was due for some better luck. And Jenny looked like she thought so too.

She watched the first pitch right onto her bat, and met it with a *ponnggggg*.

The ball shot off her bat and sailed deep into right center. Both outfielders took off after it, and they seemed to have a shot at it. They were converging, going all out. At the last second the right fielder gave way, and Villareal stretched with everything he had.

But the ball was *just beyond his reach!*

With two outs the runners had taken off with the crack of the bat. By the time the ball dropped, Jonathan was rounding third and heading home. Coach Wilkens was waving his arm, jumping up and down, sending Sterling in behind Jonathan.

But the play could be close.

Sterling was running all out. He hit the dirt hard.

The catcher might have had a chance, but the throw took a high bounce, and he had to jump for it. Sterling slid under him.

"SAAAAA-eeeeeefff!" the umpire bellowed.

Jenny played it smart. During the fury of the play at home, she tore over to third.

Jonathan cheered and then spun and ran back to Jenny. He leaped in the air and slapped her hand. "You're *TOUGH!*" he shouted.

Jenny laughed. But then she yelled, "Come on, Jacob. Bring me home!"

The game was far from over.

The score was tied, but the Dodgers needed to get the lead. The rookies would be coming up in the sixth, so now was the time to score.

Jacob was nervous. A big load was on his shoulders.

Hausberg started with a slow rainbow curve that seemed to freeze Jacob. It broke over the plate for a strike.

Jacob stepped out and took a breath. Then he heard Jenny's voice. "Jacob, you can do it."

And from the dugout everyone was yelling the same thing. He heard Jonathan's voice boom above the rest. "You're *going* to do it, Jacob."

Jacob took a fastball outside. But that was a little too obvious. Big House was setting him up for the curve again.

And when it came, Jacob was ready. He stayed in his stance, waited, and then *rocked* the ball.

Jacob had hoped for a bloop single. He hadn't swung hard. But he got every bit of the ball, and it arched into the deepest part of the park, over the center fielder's head. He had himself a stand-up double, and the Dodgers were on top.

Anthony came up next, and he got fairly good wood on the ball, but he flied out, and so that was the inning.

But the Dodgers had the lead.

They needed three outs.

Still, the Giants were tough, and they weren't going to roll over for the Dodgers.

Cooper tried to pull a fast one and bunt his way on. And it almost worked. But he popped the ball up. Henry dashed toward the ball and dove for it. It was his only chance.

Jacob, in right field, couldn't tell for a moment whether Henry had reached it. He waited.

And then the umpire's arm shot up.

One out.

Hausberg up to bat.

No one wanted to win more than big House did. He took a mighty swing and drove the ball deep to left. For a few long seconds Jacob thought the ball was going over the fence. Or worse, he was afraid, Anthony, in left field now, would drop it.

But the ball was hit high, and it floated down for an easy catch. Anthony grinned and tossed the ball back to the infield. The Dodgers—and all their fans—took a sigh of relief together.

The last batter was the substitute catcher. He never got a good look at the ball. Jonathan blazed three fastballs by him that left him standing there.

The Dodgers had pulled it out—3 to 2!

They were tied for the league lead with the Giants and the Reds.

And suddenly all the Dodgers were charging Jenny, mobbing her.

Jacob got plenty of attention too. His parents came down and congratulated him and teased him about being a star, and every player slapped his hand and thanked him for coming through.

Jenny waited until things quieted down, and then she pulled Jacob aside. "I heard you're the one who talked everyone into asking me to play."

"Not really," Jacob said, and he shrugged. "I just said it. Everyone was thinking it."

"Well, anyway, thanks. I'm glad I'm playing."

Just then Jonathan walked up to them. "You guys came through!" he said. "Way to go."

"You got it started," Jenny told him. "And you pitched great."

Jonathan looked down at the ground. Finally, he came up with something he could say—without getting too embarrassed. "When you came up to bat, all I could think was how glad I was you were back on the team."

Jacob could tell that Jenny was as embarrassed as Jonathan, so he changed the subject. "Hey, we're going all the way now. We're gong to win the championship."

"That's right," Jenny said. *All the way!*

And the whole team picked up the chant.

"All the way! All the way! All the way!" all the Dodgers started yelling.

And Jacob had no doubts at all. He knew they could do it.

BOX SCORE, GAME 15

Blue Springs Giants 2   Angel Park Dodgers 3

	ab	r	h	rbi		ab	r	h	rbi
Sanchez ss	3	0	0	0	Jie 2b	3	0	1	0
Nugent lf	3	0	1	0	White 3b	3	0	0	0
Weight 3b	2	1	1	0	Sandoval ss	3	0	1	0
Villareal cf	3	0	1	1	Swingle p	2	1	2	0
Cooper 2b	2	1	0	0	Malone cf	2	1	1	0
Hausberg p	2	0	0	0	Roper 1b	3	1	1	2
Dodero c	2	0	1	1	Scott rf	2	0	2	1
Glenn 1b	1	0	0	0	Boschi lf	2	0	0	0
Spinner rf	1	0	0	0	Bacon c	1	0	1	0
Zonn c	1	0	0	0	Ruiz lf	1	0	0	0
Waganheim 1b	1	0	0	0	Sloan c	1	0	0	0
Stevens rf	1	0	0	0	Riddle 2b	1	0	0	0
ttl	**22**	**2**	**4**	**2**		**24**	**3**	**9**	**3**

Giants 1 0 0 1 0 0—2
Dodgers 0 0 0 0 3 x—3

SECOND SEASON

League standings after five games:

(Second half of season)

Dodgers	4–1
Giants	4–1
Reds	4–1
Padres	2–3
Mariners	1–4
A's	0–5

First game scores:

Dodgers	13	Mariners	0
Giants	19	Padres	4
Reds	14	A's	1

Second game scores:

Reds	5	Dodgers	1
Giants	12	Mariners	3
Padres	7	A's	5

Third game scores:

Dodgers	4	A's	2
Giants	13	Reds	8
Padres	10	Mariners	9

Fourth game scores:

Dodgers	7	Padres	4
Giants	23	A's	1
Reds	3	Mariners	0

Fifth game scores:

Dodgers	3	Giants	2
Reds	12	Padres	2
Mariners	6	A's	4

JONATHAN SWINGLE

At-Bats	Runs	Hits	RBIs	Avg.
43	21	30	28	.698

KENNY SANDOVAL

At-Bats	Runs	Hits	RBIs	Avg.
50	22	28	19	.560

SECOND-YEAR STATISTICS
JENNY ROPER

At-Bats	Runs	Hits	RBIs	Avg.
33	9	18	18	.545

SECOND-YEAR STATISTICS

JACOB SCOTT

At-Bats	Runs	Hits	RBIs	Avg.
40	11	21	11	.525

STERLING MALONE

At-Bats	Runs	Hits	RBIs	Avg.
44	9	19	16	.432

SECOND-YEAR STATISTICS

LIAN JIE

At-Bats	Runs	Hits	RBIs	Avg.
40	8	17	7	.425

HENRY WHITE

At-Bats	Runs	Hits	RBIs	Avg.
52	17	20	3	.385

BILLY BACON

At-Bats	Runs	Hits	RBIs	Avg.
22	6	6	3	.273

HARLAN SLOAN

At-Bats	Runs	Hits	RBIs	Avg.
23	4	6	3	.261

SECOND-YEAR STATISTICS

EDDIE BOSCHI

At-Bats	Runs	Hits	RBIs	Avg.
39	7	8	1	.205

BEN RIDDLE

At-Bats	Runs	Hits	RBIs	Avg.
21	1	3	2	.143

SECOND-YEAR STATISTICS

ANTHONY RUIZ

At-Bats	Runs	Hits	RBIs	Avg.
15	0	2	0	.133

ALL-STAR OF THE MONTH

HENRY WHITE

Henry is the second batter for the Dodgers' lineup this year, and he does exactly what the second batter's supposed to do: he gets on base. As a fourth grader last year—when he was the lead-off batter—he led the team with a .514 batting average. He rarely hits the long ball, but he hits singles and doubles and lets other batters bring him home. And because he has great speed, he often scores from second or even first when most players would have to hold up at third. Last year he led the team in runs scored, with 26, and he's leading the way again this year.

On defense, Henry plays third base. He earned that position as a fourth grader because of his strong, accurate arm. But he hasn't always thrown so well. In his first year in Little League, he really struggled making that long throw to first. That's when his dad and his older brother, a high school baseball star, came to the rescue. His dad hit hundreds of ground balls to Henry every week. Henry fielded the balls and then threw to his brother, who covered first base. And the practice paid off. Henry is now one of the best third basemen in the league.

When baseball is over, Henry plays soccer, and he's competed in some Junior Olympics events as well. He's a sprinter, and he plans to take up hurdles when he gets older. His brother is an excellent hurdler, and Henry thinks he might have the talent to follow in his footsteps. Some players don't like to be compared with their big brothers or sisters, but Henry doesn't mind. He doesn't feel any competition with him, since the two are such good friends.

Henry is a quiet boy, both on and off the field. At school, a person would never guess that he was an athlete. He seems to have his nose in a book all the time. He even reads during lunch, and his mother complains because he doesn't like to go to bed at night. It's always "Just a couple more pages" when she wants him to get to sleep. But then, maybe that's partly her fault, since she's an English teacher and has set the pattern for lots of reading in her home.

Henry's father is a sales representative for a computer company. He spends a lot of time traveling, but when he's home, he often has more time to be with his sons than most fathers do. And he adjusts his schedule so that he can attend their games. That isn't always easy, with the many sports they play, but he gets to all the games he can. And Henry's mother also knows sports inside and out. She's usually up in the bleachers shouting advice when Henry is up to bat.

With one more year left in Little League, Henry is likely to be a very big star. He's growing all the time, and some of those singles are going to start turning into extra-base hits, or even home runs. Look for big things from this young man in baseball, soccer, and track—and in anything he sets out to do in life. He has the quiet confidence to be anything he wants to be.

DEAN HUGHES has written many books for children, including the popular *Nutty* stories and *Jelly's Circus*. He has also published such works of literary fiction for young adults as the highly acclaimed *Family Pose*. Writing keeps Mr. Hughes very busy, but he does find time to run and play golf—and he loves to watch almost all sports. His home is in Utah. He and his wife have three children, all in college.